Copyright © 1996 by Educational Publishing Concepts, Inc., Wheaton, Illinois

Published by Concordia Publishing House
3558 S. Jefferson Avenue, St. Louis, MO 63118-3968
Manufactured in the United States of America

1 2 3 4 5 6 7 8 9 10   05 04 03 02 01 00 99 98 97 96

God's Creative World

Kathryn E. Nielson
Illustrated by Rick Incrocci

CPH
SAINT LOUIS

Wasn't God creative when
He gave us all our days,
Seven in a week
To live and work and play?

And wasn't He creative when
He made the deep, dark night—
A time to rest and gain relief
From our full and busy life?

Wasn't God creative when
He made the big blue sky—
A great expanse to separate
The waters low and high?

Wasn't God creative when
He made the deep blue sea,
So we can swim and sail,
And fish for food to eat?

And wasn't He creative when
He formed the different trees
With leaves to hold the raindrops,
And branches to catch the breeze?

Wasn't God creative when
He made the moon to rise,
To guide us through the darkness,
By lighting up the skies?

And wasn't He creative when
He made the sun so bright,
To welcome each new morning,
And disappear each night?

Wasn't God creative when
He made the birds to sing—
To fill the air with music
With their return in spring?

Wasn't God creative when
He filled up all the land
With different kinds of animals
Uniquely named by man?

And wasn't He creative when
He formed us from the dust,
To worship, serve, and praise Him,
Until with Him we rest?

God looked at all that He had done—
The world that He had made.
"It is good," He gladly said,
And rested on this day.

So this is how the world began—
From God's creative hand;
The earth and stars and sea and sky
Came at His great command.